THE
№1 CAR
SPOTTER
and the Firebird

Books by Atinuke:

Anna Hibiscus

Hooray for Anna Hibiscus!

Good Luck, Anna Hibiscus!

Have Fun, Anna Hibiscus!

The No. 1 Car Spotter

The No. 1 Car Spotter and the Firebird

For younger readers:

Anna Hibiscus' Song

THE No1 CAR SPOTTER

and the Firebird

by Atinuke

illustrated by Warwick Johnson Cadwell

Kane Miller

A DIVISION OF EDC PUBLISHING

First American Edition 2012
Kane Miller, A Division of EDC Publishing

Text © 2011 by Atinuke
Illustrations © 2011 by Warwick Johnson Cadwell

For information contact:
Kane Miller, A Division of EDC Publishing
P.O. Box 470663
Tulsa, OK 74147-0663
www.kanemiller.com
www.edcpub.com

Library of Congress Control Number: 2010943436

Printed and bound in the United States of America
1 2 3 4 5 6 7 8 9 10
ISBN: 978-1-61067-052-4

For my father
A.

To my gang once again,
D, S, H and W
W. JC.

No. 1 and the Slingshot

My name is Oluwalase Babatunde Benson. But everybody calls me No. 1. I am the No. 1 car spotter. The No. 1 car spotter in my village.

In my village we do not have television, or even electricity. We do not have shops, or even traffic lights.

We have our compounds, where we live.
We have our farms, where we work. We
have the river, where we play. And best
of all we have the road that runs past the
village, carrying buses and trucks and cars
from one city to another.

And I am the No. 1 car spotter. I know
the cars before I see them by the sound of
their engines, sweet or backfiring. I call their
names before they even appear.
That is why they call me No. 1!
I can spot one now!
"Firebird!" I shout.
The Firebird passes in a whirlwind of
dust. It is a red speck leading the tornado.

I stop splashing with my best friend,
Coca-Cola, to watch. Uncle Go-Easy stops
mending his nets to watch. His boys,
Tuesday and Emergency, stop hoeing the
fields to watch. Even Grandfather stops his
fly whisk to watch.

All this stop stopping of our work annoys the women. Because car spotting is something it takes a man to understand.

"Why are the goats not in the bush?" Grandmother suddenly shouts.

"No. 1!" Mama calls. "You who are so quick to shout and so slow to work! O-ya!"

"Coca-Cola! Take the goats with No. 1!" shouts Coca-Cola's mother.

Coca-Cola and I both groan. We are swimming in the cool river. Now we will have to trek into the hot-hot bush.

"That is where car spotting gets you," says my sister, Sissy. And she and her best friend, Nike, laugh.

We only have time to narrow our eyes at them before we run. Already all the women in the village are releasing their goats from their compounds. We must escort the goats to the bush where they look for food, and we keep them from becoming lost.

The bush is hot. There is no shade.
The air is like oil on the road. Suddenly
something moves.

"Snake!" I shout.

Coca-Cola pulls out his slingshot. *Ping!*
The big snake reverses fast into the bush.

"You see that, No. 1!" Coca-Cola crows.

"Good one," I say. It is too hot to say
more.

Coca-Cola hits a small rock. He hits a bush.
He hits a leaf. My slingshot does not leave
my pocket.

When we return to the village, Coca-Cola boasts. "I dispatch one big-big snake double-triple quick!"

"What about you, No. 1?" Sissy asks.

"I could have hit a leopard with one shot," I say.

"No. 1!" Sissy laughs. "You think you fit chase off leopard?"

Everybody laughs at me. I scratch the ground with my foot. Sissy, Nike, Coca-Cola, Emergency and Tuesday take out their slingshots. They practice hitting small stones.

I look away. I see something.

"Firebird!" I shout.

On the road a tiny speeding something is growing bigger. Soon the something is clearly red. The Firebird zooms back past the village!

Sissy, Nike, Coca-Cola, Emergency and
Tuesday are now talking about when they
will be big hunters. How the village will sing
their praise songs.

"Of course, you will all be big hunters,"
I join in. "You will eat meat every day. And
when I pass you in my big car, listening to
my big stereo on my way from one big city
to another, I will honk my horn and wave
to you."

I run to join Grandfather under the iroko
tree before they can answer.

Grandfather is always
under the iroko tree. It is his
place as an old man.
To sit in the only
shade in the village
where he can observe
everything and
everybody without
tiring his neck.

"You see that Firebird?" Grandfather asks me when I sit down. "A No. 1 car! And it is the only one in our country!"

I say nothing. Grandfather looks over at Sissy and the others. They are hitting a small rock with their slingshots. This is not something I can do. Grandfather sighs.

"Nobody is good at everything, No. 1," he says. "You are the No. 1 car spotter. That is enough."

But it is not enough to stop the others laughing at me.

Grandfather and I watch the road together. We call the names of the cars softly so as not to annoy the women. They are cooking. We are hungry. Soon it is time to eat.

That very night, when the village is sleeping, all the goats start to bleat. Their voices are high and loud and frightened.

Uncle Go-Easy's voice shouts out.
Then Mama Coca-Cola's. We jump up
from our mats. There is silence.
Slowly we lie back down.

In the morning we gather under
the iroko tree to hear
what has happened
in the night.

"A leopard! A great spotted leopard!"
Uncle Go-Easy's voice shakes.

A leopard had visited his compound. It
tried to take a goat, but the speedy slingshot
of Tuesday deterred it. Then it went to
Mama Coca-Cola's compound, where it
succeeded. Now she has one less goat.

"This boy was
sleeping." Mama
Coca-Cola shakes
Coca-Cola by his
ear. "Where was
his slingshot?"

Our compound
walls are not strong. They are made of
brushwood, rotting planks and clay. Strong
enough to pen goats in, but not strong
enough to keep leopards out.

Usually leopards like to keep as far from
us as we do from them. It is a mutual
understanding.

"This one must be old," says Grandfather.

"Or sick," says Grandmother.

Too old or sick to hunt. And our goats are easy prey.

"The last time a leopard came we got rid of it," Mama says.

"We had a whole village full of people then," Grandmother sighs.

"We lit torches and ran out of our houses, shouting and banging drums," Grandfather explains. "The leopard ran away."

"Now what will we do?" asks Auntie Fine-Fine. "Everybody is in the city, and there are not enough of us left to frighten a leopard away."

"My goats will die-o! All of them!" wails Mama Coca-Cola. "Then I will be poor! Poor!"

"We have our slingshots," says Tuesday.

"It is true!" agrees Uncle Go-Easy. "Tuesday succeeded in frightening off the leopard with his slingshot last night!"

For a while there is silence. Then Grandfather speaks. "Let nobody go alone to the bush or the farm until this trouble is resolved," he says. "We will send word around to the other villages. They will come to help us chase the leopard away. Until then the children can fire their slingshots, but only from the windows!"

Everybody nods in agreement.

I am glad Sissy is in my compound to fire slingshot. If the leopard was as big as an elephant, I would not be able to hit it.

"But what about me?" wails Mama B. "I have no child in the house that can fire slingshot! The leopard will take all my goats."

It is true. Mama B's children are small.

"You can have Sissy," Mama says quickly.

I look at Mama wide-eyed, but I say
nothing. It is organized that every compound
has a child old enough to shoot a slingshot.
Sissy goes to Mama B. And that leaves only
me to protect our compound.

That night I wait by the window.
I fire a stone from my slingshot.
It hits the wall. It does not
even exit the window.
Now it is
Mama who
looks at me
wide-eyed.

Suddenly a leopard screams. Triumphant shouts come from Mama Coca-Cola's compound. Our goats bleat loud and frightened. Grandmother wakes.

"Shoot, No. 1!" she shouts. "Shoot!"

 A stone shoots from my slingshot and exits the window. Hooray! Then a goat squeals in answer, and Mama snatches the slingshot from me.

"Do you want to join the leopard in killing our goats!" Mama shouts.

Grandmother turns to Grandfather. He has his eyes tight shut.

"The leopard is stealing our goats, and this boy can do nothing!" she screams.

"I am sleeping-o!" Grandfather mutters crossly. "Can an old man not sleep in his own house? The boy is old enough to look after things."

Mama turns away from the window. "The leopard has just taken one of our goats," she says.

Grandmother cries.

The following day Mama and Grandmother and I try to strengthen the compound walls. Sissy comes to help us. We bring more brushwood. That night the leopard comes again. This time my hands shake so badly I drop the stones. The leopard carries off another goat.

The following night as we are eating, Grandmother wails.

"This boy is useless. Usless! We must ask Sissy to return."

We all look hopefully at Grandfather. He dips his cassava dough eba in some hot chili pepper soup and lifts it to his mouth.

"And leave Mama B alone with three babies?" he asks. He shakes his head. Unthinkable.

So our goats will soon be gone. Our family will sink into poverty. And it will be all my fault.

I stretch out my hand to dip my eba into the stew. But I am thinking about our goats, and I make a mistake. My hand copies Grandfather's and dips into the hot chili pepper soup instead. Immediately I put the eba in my mouth, I am on fire.

"ARRRRRGGGHHH!!!!!!!!!"

Grandmother and Grandfather are fond of the soup made of ground chili peppers, but children cannot eat it. One has to get used to it gradually, over years and years.

I run to the bucket and pour water into my mouth. Still my lips and tongue and throat are on fire.

Mama milks a goat. Grandfather pours milk into my mouth. Gradually the flames die down, but the embers are still burning.

Grandmother sucks her teeth.

"Soon there will be no goats to save you from your own mistakes," she says. "Why do you not make the leopard run and scream like you?"

I look at Grandmother. Losing goats is making her mean. But her words have given me a No. 1 idea!

When everybody goes into the house to sleep I take one of Grandfather's old shirts that is outside drying. I fold the shirt and tie it tight around a goat. The goat bleats angrily.

"What is happening with that goat?" Mama's voice calls.

"I am collecting more milk for my throat," I answer hoarsely.

I take the soup pot. Quickly I smear the chili pepper soup onto the shirt tied around the goat. The folded cloth prevents the paste from touching the goat's skin. But still

she bleats, annoyed. I tie her quickly to the
fence. She bleats again.

"No. 1! Leave that goat and come inside!"
Mama calls again.

I go inside and lie down on my mat.
I close my eyes. No more waiting at the
window with my slingshot for me.

"Useless boy," Grandmother says.

In the middle of the night our goats begin to bleat. I recognize each one. Louder than all the others is the goat that is annoyed at wearing a shirt and being tied to the fence. I hear the creak of brushwood. The leopard is pushing its way into our compound!

I leap from my mat and press my face against the window. Let it choose the goat that is bleating so loud! Let it choose the one that cannot run!

I see the leopard spring. Then I hear it howl. It chose the right goat! Now it has tasted chili pepper. My plan has succeeded!

Grandfather, Grandmother and Mama leap up and press their faces to the window. The leopard is rolling on the ground. I know the pain exactly. My own mouth is still hot.

"Sorry-o," I whisper.

"Sorry what!" shouts Grandmother. "What happen?"

"The leopard swallow pepper soup," I say.

Everybody looks at me.

"Pepper soup?" says Mama.

"I put pepper soup onto a shirt," I say.
"And I put the shirt onto a goat."

"You did what!" shouts Grandmother.

"The leopard tried to swallow that goat,
but he swallow pepper soup first," I conclude.

Grandmother, Grandfather and Mama
look back at the leopard. It is still rolling
on the ground.

Suddenly the leopard leaps up. It crashes
through
the fence
and races
away
into the
night.

The goat is running around the compound, still alive! And still wearing Grandfather's shirt!

Mama starts to laugh. She laughs so hard she cannot stop. Grandfather and Grandmother are laughing too.

"That leopard will not want to taste goat again," Mama says at last.

"And it will never enter a village again," chuckles Grandfather.

"I knew this boy was cleva!" Grandmother announces. "He is a cleva-cleva boy!"

"You said he was useless." Mama is still laughing.

"With the slingshot that is true!" answers Grandmother.

"There is no need to be good with slingshot," Grandfather says loudly, "when you have a No. 1 brain! Tomorrow we will tell your sister and those other big hunters how you chased away a leopard without using even a slingshot."

That will stop them laughing at me, I thought.

I smile my No. 1 smile. I am No. 0 at slingshot, but I am the No. 1 car spotter. And I am No. 1 at chasing away leopards too!

No. 1 and the Flood

In my village Sissy is No. 1 at school, Coca-Cola is No. 1 at counting, Tuesday is No. 1 at slingshot, Emergency is No. 1 at running, Nike is No. 1 at catching chickens, and I am the No. 1 car spotter.

Grandfather says there is no need to be No. 1 at more than one thing. That way we need one another. Call it cooperation. Call it friendship. If we were all No. 1 at everything we would no longer have any use for each other. And then what would be the point of being a human race?

All I wish is that the Firebird would co-
operate with me. I am the No. 1 car spotter.
And the Pontiac Firebird is the No. 1 car on
our road. But I have never taken a good look
at it. The professor who drives it has never
stopped in our village.

Sissy thinks this does not matter. And
Nike agrees. But they are girls. What do they
know?

For Grandfather and Uncle Go-Easy and
the others, it is enough that such a No. 1 car
passes through our village.

I know that the day the Firebird stops here
would be the No. 1 of all No. 1 days.

I am looking for dry firewood. In the
rainy season it is hard to find. When it
rains day and night everything is wet. But
Grandmother has told me not to come back
to the compound without dry wood. How
else is she supposed to cook my food?

"No. 1! No. 1! No. 1!" Sissy is shouting. She went this morning to the river to wash clothes. When I look, I see Sissy and Nike are on the big rock. They like to wash clothes on this rock. It is on the edge of the water. Between the road and the river. You can climb the rock without getting your feet wet.

But now I see it is
surrounded by water on
every side. All this rain has caused the river
to swell. And here, where the road runs
alongside the river, it is beginning to flood.
I start to run.

"No. 1! Hurry up!" Nike shouts.

The river is not running fast. Sissy and
Nike can both swim, but not with baskets
full of wet clothes. If we lose those clothes,
we will have only the ones we are wearing.
I prepare myself to swim to the rock and
help Sissy and Nike.

But when I enter the water it does not
even reach my knees. The girls jump off
the rock and wade back to the road.
I laugh at them.

"Did you call me because you
were afraid to wet your feet?" I ask.

"We did not see the water rise,"
Sissy says.

"It could have been deep!" says Nike.

Of course they are right. And as we stand there the river swells more. Soon it has covered the whole road. The water is not moving fast. It looks like a small lake.

"Honda!" Coca-Cola shouts from the village.

The driver brakes when she comes around the corner and sees the flooded road. But when she notices that the water is only ankle-deep, she drives through.

"Ford!" shouts Grandfather under the iroko tree.

"Peugeot!" shouts Emergency in the yam fields.

When the drivers see the flood, they too slow down and slowly-slowly pass. But the river continues to rise. Now it has reached my knees. It is as high as the foothold on the big rock.

"Limousine!" shouts Coca-Cola.

"BMW!" Emergency shouts.

The cars brake sharp on the edge of the
flood. They look at the water swirling
around our knees.

A big woman in an embroidered buba
and wrappa gets out of the back of the
limousine. A man in a sharp-sharp American
suit gets out of the BMW. They greet each
other loudly.

"Mammy-wagon!" calls Coca-Cola.

The mammy-wagon stops too. The bus driver climbs down. His passengers follow him, all looking agitated.

"O-ya! What now?" shouts a big man. "We are already late for our daughter's wedding because of your go-slow bus! Continue!"

"Oga-sir," begs the bus driver. "That water will quench my engine-o."

"You are making excuses!" shouts one of the women.

"We will miss the wedding. We will miss it-o!" the passengers wail.

"No. 1! No. 1!" Grandfather is shouting from the village. "What happen there?"

I turn and run back. As I run past Mama Coca-Cola's akara stall I shout: "The river done flood! The road is blocked! The cars cannot pass!"

Mama Coca-Cola's eyes shine. She puts four frying pans on the fire and calls to Mama B and Auntie Fine-Fine.

"Come and help me here! Come, my sisters-o! We will make money today!"

I run up to the iroko tree. I tell Grandfather about the flood.

"Let us go!" says Grandfather.

Down at the flood all the people from the bus are crying and shouting into their mobile phones. I can see another bus on the other side of the water. It too has passengers who are waving their arms and shouting. The water is still no higher than the foothold on the rock, no deeper than my knee. But that

is too deep for a car or bus to pass. These
people are going nowhere.

Then I see something that makes me jump
for joy. The Firebird. The fabulous Pontiac
Firebird. It is approaching the flood. It will
stop! At last it has to stop!

"Firebird!" I say to Grandfather.

He straightens his hat and straightens his
back. I am dancing and jumping for joy.

The Firebird stops. There is only one person inside. It must be the professor. Grandfather has told me all about university professors. He has explained the whole thing to me.

"There are businessmen in this country, and there are politicians. Most of them corrupt. They are only interested in getting richer and richer!" he had said.

"Then there are those who help others. They have nothing dodgy going on. They put nothing into their pockets that belong to others. That is why we call them NGO, Nothing Going On. Like our own NGO, who gave us the wheelbarrows.

"The ones who teach the teachers and the doctors and the NGOs, those are the university professors! And the man who drives the Firebird?

He is one of those. A university professor."

I have never seen a university professor. Will he look like a politician in the embroidered robes of a chief or a business-man in a sharp-sharp American suit?

The door of the Firebird opens. A short man comes out and frowns at the flood.

He is not dressed like an American.

He is not dressed like a chief.

He is dressed like an ordinary man.

In traditional trousers and long matching shirt. Only the cloth that is new and fine shows he is not a poor man.

43

"Prof!" calls the chief from the limousine. "Don't tell me now that we politicians don't need our private planes!"

"Prof!" calls the businessman from the BMW. "How we can do business in this country when nobody repairs the roads?"

The people from the bus all turn to look at the people calling from their fine-fine cars.

"Can't you help us, madam chief?" One of the women begs the woman in the limousine.

Suddenly my mouth opens. Without consulting my brain.

"The water is not too deep," I say. "Why do you not walk to the other side?"

There is a short silence. The rich people laugh, and the wedding people start to shout.

"You want us to spoil our clothes!"

"And arrive at the wedding looking like dogs!"

"Who asked you to talk to us? Were we talking to you?"

I look at the ground. My skin is crawling with shame.

"Whose foolish boy is this?" asks the lady chief.

A hand grips my arm.

"This is my boy, my No. 1 boy," says Grandfather. "Give him a problem, and he will find a No. 1 solution."

The professor raises his eyebrows. The rich businessman and the chief laugh. The people from the bus suck their teeth. What can a small boy like me do to solve a problem as big as this?

"These people cannot walk," Grandfather says to me. "You must use your No. 1 brain to find another solution."

But my brain is away from its desk. It has resigned. Everybody laughs as I run away.

I run behind our compound and hide underneath the village Cow-rolla.

Once I was a boy who achieved electricity for brain. I turned a broken-down car into this fine Cow-rolla. I made Grandfather proud. But a Cow-rolla is not the answer to everything. Or is it?

Electric flash for brain! I jump over the wall into our compound.

"What are you doing?" shouts Grandmother. "Trying to give me a heart attack?"

I do not answer. I yoke the cows. I lead them from the compound.

"Where are you going with those cows? No. 1, answer me!" Grandmother is still shouting.

But the current is running, and there is no off switch. Without answering I hitch the cows to the Cow-rolla and lead them away.

Grandmother is looking over the compound wall.

"Nobody will marry that boy. He is too much initiative-initiative," she grumbles.

"He will never listen to his wife."

I take the cows straight to the river. Now there are many cars and buses and people stopped on both sides of the flood. A little to one side is Grandfather.

As soon as he sees me, Grandfather smiles. Then he jumps up and shouts,

"Make way! Make way for the No. 1 river transport!"

Grandfather's hat falls into the water and the river carries it away, but he does not notice. He is too busy shouting and waving his arms. Enjoying watching people's faces as they turn and see me arrive with the Cow-rolla.

"My No. 1 boy will take all of you to the other side of the water. The buses there can take you on your way." Grandfather shouts, "Show them, No. 1!"

I lead the Cow-rolla into the flood. The water only reaches the knees of the cows. There is no current. They are ready to cross.

Everybody is cheering and unloading their bags and baggages from the buses. The big men from the fine-fine cars push their way to the front.

"What about us?" they ask. "How will we get our cars across?"

"Sorry," says Grandfather, "we only have public transportation solutions here. People with private cars and private airplanes have to find their own way. Unless you want to take the bus?"

The men go back to their cars. It is then that I see the Firebird is gone. The professor must have turned around to leave the way he came. He saw me run in shame. Did he see me return? I turn to Grandfather.

"Forty naira per person," Grandfather is saying loudly to the people pushing to get onto the Cow-rolla. "Twenty naira per bag."

People argue and complain, but Grandfather refuses to move from the price.

"First you call my grandson foolish, you laugh at him and insult him. And now you want him to carry you back and forth, back and forth for nothing?"

Grandfather sucks his teeth. "No chance."

People dig into their pockets.

Those going to the wedding are the quickest to pay. I lead them across the flood on the back of the Cow-rolla. There they enter one of the buses waiting and go on their way.

I come back carrying people who want to go this way.

For many hours I lead the Cow-rolla through the water, back and forth. Sometimes my friend Coca-Cola walks with me. Sometimes my sister Sissy. They smile big smiles and wave to the people clicking us on mobile phones.

Grandfather collects handful after handful of notes. Grandmother cries with joy as she counts the notes at the end of the day.

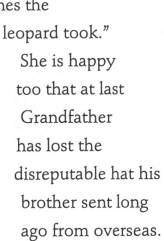

"We will buy many-many more good fat strong goats with this money!" Grandmother says. "To replace the ones the leopard took."

She is happy too that at last Grandfather has lost the disreputable hat his brother sent long ago from overseas.

The whole village comes to celebrate our wealth with us. Mama Coca-Cola too has made enough money to replace the goat the leopard took from her.

I hear many shouts of joy from my compound and from the whole village.

"Well done, No. 1! Well-done-o!"

That is what I hear.

It makes me happy. But what of the professor, what does he think of me?

Mama Coca-Cola's New House

I am the No. 1, and my best friend is Coca-Cola.

As you already know, Coca-Cola's mother, Mama Coca-Cola, runs the akara stall on the road. She cooks the best black-eyed pea akara fritters I have ever tasted. Buses, taxis, cars – many of them stop to buy Mama Coca-Cola's sweet akara. The stall is a good place to spot cars.

"Firebird!" Coca-Cola yells. He looks at me. "Come now. Shout!"

I say nothing. The Firebird passes, spraying water from the puddles on the road.

Mama Coca-Cola sucks her teeth.

"I will have to go and find plastic to cover this akara," she says. "When will this rainy season finish?"

I go to sit with Grandfather under the iroko tree. Together we watch the cars and buses drive past, spraying water everywhere. It is raining again.

Then Mama Coca-Cola's voice shouts from her house. "Bucket! Quick! Bring me bucket!"

I look at Grandfather.

"Go! Go!" he says.

I run to our compound and snatch Grandmother's buckets. I run to Coca-Cola's compound through the rain. Water is pouring through the roof of Mama Coca-Cola's house. Mama Coca-Cola is rushing around trying to cover sacks of peas with small pieces of plastic.

"My peas!" she is shouting. "My peas will spoil!"

This is serious. How can Mama Coca-Cola cook akara without peas? And how will she feed her family if she does not sell akara?

Coca-Cola and I go to every compound in the village begging for buckets. Mama, Grandmother, Mama B, Auntie Fine-Fine, Uncle Go-Easy and everybody comes to help. All that day we fight the rain. Moving buckets around the house, chasing the leaks that jump from one place to another.

At last the rain stops. It is already night. Time to cook and sleep. Grandmother and Auntie Fine-Fine stretch and groan.

"Collect the buckets," Mama says to me.

"Let us go," says Mama B.

"Wait!" Mama Coca-Cola shouts. "Where are you going? I need those buckets! What will I do when the rain comes again?"

"You cannot expect our buckets to remain here throughout the rainy season!" Grandmother answers.

"My children are hungry, and I need
to cook," says Mama B. "I need to wash
my vegetables, soak my peas and clean
my yam. I need my buckets, sister."

Grandfather arrives at Mama Coca-Cola's
compound.

He asks crossly, "Am I the only one in this
village whose stomach knows it is time to
chop?"

"She has our buckets!" Auntie Fine-Fine
complains.

"They want my house to fall down and my
peas to spoil!" Mama Coca-Cola shouts.

Grandfather sighs. He listens to
everybody. Then he looks at Mama
Coca-Cola's house.

It is a traditional house with palm
leaf roof and round clay walls.
But now it is old and
cracked and leaky.

"The village must build Mama Coca-Cola a new house," Grandfather says at last.

It takes a whole village to build a house. It means women and girls digging and stamping and shaping mud into bricks for many long days. It means men and boys climbing and cutting and carrying and fixing sharp palm fronds for the roof. It means finding and stirring and mixing the exact traditional recipe for the plaster. It means everybody else cooking and cooking and cooking for those who are working so hard.

The whole village groans.

"There are not enough of us to build a house," Grandmother complains. "It takes a full village."

"Still, a house needs to be built," says Grandfather.

We all look at Mama Coca-Cola's house. Traditional houses cannot last, last, last. Not like the modern buildings I see in the town on market days. Nothing can wash away cement. Nothing can nibble away concrete. It does not crack. It is hard like iron.

"We cannot build now anyway," says Uncle Go-Easy. "If we build before the dry season comes, the rain will wash the clay bricks away."

"Then I must keep your buckets!" Mama Coca-Cola says crossly.

I clear my throat. Nobody looks at me. So I open my mouth and say, "If we build a modern house from cement blocks, then we can begin at once. And it will never leak."

"No. 1! Be quiet!" says Mama.

Children are not allowed to enter the conversations of their seniors. Especially not when serious matters are being discussed.

"Anyway, modern houses are expensive," says Grandmother.

"Too expensive for village people!" says Uncle Go-Easy.

Everybody nods. Then Grandfather says, "Mama Coca-Cola and her peas must stay with Mama B until the dry season. Then we can build her another house. Now, everybody, take your buckets and go and cook!"

So Mama Coca-Cola moves her family and all her belongings, including her sacks of peas, to her sister, Mama B's, house. And we all return to our own compounds with our buckets.

In the morning I can spot the road from where I am busy picking palm nuts high in the palm trees.

Mama Coca-Cola is busy at the akara stall. She is busy, not only frying akara, but also collecting money from every customer that owes her.

"Pay my money or else no more akara! No more!" I can hear her shout at every car, bus, truck and taxi that stops.

Commuters, truck drivers, taxi drivers, I see everybody pay. Once a person has tasted Mama Coca-Cola's akara, who can live without it?

When Mama Coca-Cola has finished collecting her money, she enters a taxi and sets off for the town. When she returns in the evening, Mama Coca-Cola is smiling wider than she has ever smiled before.

Now Mama Coca-Cola borrows mobile phone from everybody she knows who stops at the stall. She shouts loud and long into those phones. Until the day a big truck arrives and parks behind the akara stall.

The truck is full of men and a lot of building materials. There are sacks of cement and plaster and sand. There are  many-many concrete blocks. I quickly climb down from the palm tree, drop the nuts, and run to the road.

The whole village is gathered there staring at the modern expensive materials being unloaded right next to the akara stall. Mama Coca-Cola's smile is breaking her face.

"What is happening here?" Grandmother is puffing and panting.

"I am building a house," Mama Coca-Cola announces. "A fine *modern* house. Four concrete walls, four corners, iron roof, concrete floor. No more leaks. No more rain. Modern house, convenient life!"

Mama Coca-Cola looks at me.

"A No. 1 idea!" she says.

Grandmother sighs and shakes her head. She walks back to our compound.

"When you find a way for clothes to wash themselves, call me," she says over her shoulder. "Until then I am too busy for all this!"

I present myself to the builders. After all, this was my No. 1 idea, and I am now ready to take part. But the builders laugh and shake their heads.

"This is not for small boys," they say. "Modern expertise is needed to build modern house."

The whole village laughs.

"No. 1!" Grandmother shouts from our compound. "I need firewood."

I pick up the sticks one by one as I watch those annoying ye-ye builders. They are clearing and digging the ground. What kind of modern expertise is that?

"No. 1!" shouts Grandmother. "Do you want to eat today or tomorrow?"

I return with the wood and stop under the iroko tree. Grandfather too is watching the builders. Now they are mixing powder from the sacks with water and sand to make a paste. I have helped to make a clay paste to build a traditional house.

"I can do that," I say to Grandfather.

"Concentrate on firewood," says Grandfather. "I want to eat today."

When I drop the firewood, Mama sends me to the river to water the cows. Uncle Go-Easy is there. Together we watch the house walls being built from big concrete blocks. The blocks are fixed together using the paste. We too use our clay paste to fix together small clay bricks.

"I can do that," I say.

"That is modern business," says Uncle Go-Easy. "Go easy, No. 1."

"And it is men's work," says Sissy, busy washing clothes. "Are you a man now?"

I narrow my eyes at Sissy, but I say nothing more until later, when I am alone with Coca-Cola. It is siesta time. Everybody has returned to the compounds to eat and sleep. The builders are in Mama B's compound being fed by Mama Coca-Cola. Even Grandfather is absent from under the iroko tree.

"I can do everything those men are doing!" I say to Coca-Cola. "I can build your mother's house."

Coca-Cola looks at me with wide eyes. "You are truly the No. 1!" he says.

And Coca-Cola is truly my best friend.

"O-ya, come on!" I say.

Coca-Cola follows me down to the building site. There is a sack of white powder already open.

"Fetch water!" I say. "Pour!"

Coca-Cola tips a whole bucket of water onto the open sack. The powder flies up into the air and covers Coca-Cola and me from head to toe. All of a sudden we are white!

"Oyinbo!" I laugh at Coca-Cola. "White boy!"

Coca-Cola laughs too and pours more water onto the powder. The water sticks the powder to our feet. We begin to tread. This is the traditional way of forming a paste, mixing it with our feet. But there is too much water here. It runs along the ground, washing the powder away. I take another sack and empty it onto the mixture.

"We must work hard," I say to Coca-Cola, "and finish your mother's house before those lazy men wake up."

Coca-Cola and I work hard. But somehow the paste does not form well. And it is aggravating our feet. Burning them.

"Let us go to the river to wash," I groan. Coca-Cola agrees miserably.

Before we can go anywhere, my mother comes out of our compound. She takes one look at us and starts to scream. The whole village wakes up.

"No. 1! No. 1!" Mama wails. "Is that you?"

"It is him," says Sissy. "I recognize the shorts."

"Coca-Cola!" screams Mama Coca-Cola. "What has happened to my boy?"

Coca-Cola is crying, "My feet! My feet!"

I am crying too. I cannot move ankle or toe.

Emergency runs to wake the sleeping builders.

When they see Coca-Cola and me they laugh.  They carry us down to the river.

The river washes the powdery cement easily off our bodies. But the cement that has hardened remains on our feet, burning our skin. The builders reassure us that eventually it will wear off. Our feet will only be white temporarily. But in the meantime our feet will pain us, and Mama Coca-Cola will have to order some more materials to replace what we have wasted.

Mama Coca-Cola swings her handbag in the direction of Coca-Cola. Now she knows that Coca-Cola will live, she is angry.

"Now I will have to find more money!" she shouts. "Who told you to go and mix cement?"

"No. 1!" answers Coca-Cola sorrowfully.

"And if No. 1 told you to jump from a cliff, would you jump?" Mama Coca-Cola swings her bag at me.

"Just leave my boy alone!" shouts Mama.

Emergency carries me to sit under the iroko tree. Coca-Cola is brought there crying. Grandmother brings us ogi porridge and other sweet things to eat. She orders our mothers and all of the aunties not to ask me or Coca-Cola to do any work whatsoever. Because it might cause the cement to glue itself permanently to our feet.

"If those boys' feet are still white when they grow up NOBODY will marry them," Grandmother says.

I look at Coca-Cola. The pain in my feet is so bad, but if it means nobody will marry me, then I am happy. "Don't worry," I say to Coca-Cola. The food is good, the shade under the tree is pleasant, the company is superb, and there is an excellent view of the road… "Honda!" I shout happily.

Coca-Cola stops crying. He too looks at the road.

"Peugeot!" he shouts.

Sissy passes with a load of firewood on her head.

"Lazy boys!" she says.

I ignore her. After all I am the No. 1 car spotter. And right now I am busy. Busy doing what I do best!

The No. 1 Chop-House

From where I sit under the iroko tree with Grandfather and Coca-Cola, I can keep my eye on everything. Coca-Cola and I still have cement on our feet, but not much. The burning has stopped. The pain has lessened. And I am still the No. 1 car spotter, spotting not only cars!

Down on the road Mama Coca-Cola's new house meets in four corners, just as Mama Coca-Cola has requested.

Grandmother sucks her teeth.

"Does Mama Coca-Cola not know that dirt likes to hide in corner-corner?"

But it is too late for discussion. The builders are already attaching the strong sheets of corrugated iron roof.

"No more leaking! You see that iron? That is solid iron between me and the rain!" Mama Coca-Cola is so happy.

But Grandfather shakes his head. "I have seen many-many iron roofs with rust hole like colander admitting the rain. It is only a matter of time!"

But Mama Coca-Cola dances when her roof is completed. And claps as the builders plaster the walls inside and out.

"Why that white nonsense?" Grandfather asks. "Is our traditional plaster not good enough?"

But it is too late to argue. Mama Coca-Cola's house is finished! She is calling friends and family from all over the area to celebrate. It is up to the village to provide a good feast.

From under the iroko tree we see Sissy pushing wheelbarrows of soft drinks and carrying sacks of peas ready for the party.

"Lazy-lazy boys," she hisses at us.

When I am alone I find that I can wiggle my toes. And Coca-Cola and I even enjoyed a game of football when everybody was away at market. Just for rehabilitation. But right now I am too busy spotting the cars of all Mama Coca-Cola's relatives and friends to answer Sissy.

At the party Coca-Cola and I are given good seats next to Grandfather. We are served good food. Amala and ewedu, Grandfather's favorite. Pounded yam and goat stew, Coca-Cola's favorite. Jollof rice and fried chicken, my favorite. I eat them all!

"Not too lazy to eat," Sissy hisses.

When the drums start, people begin to dance. And I look down, and suddenly I see my feet begin to move. I try to hide them under Grandfather's stool. But the drums continue, getting louder.

Before I know what I am doing, my feet enter the dance floor. Up and down and around they dance. Jumping and stamping, crouching and leaping high!

"No. 1! No. 1!" Mama and Grandmother are cheering. "Our boy is cured!"

"Coca-Cola!" Mama Coca-Cola shouts happily. "Coca-Cola!"

Coca-Cola is there, dancing beside me.
We dance so well that the drummers drum
louder and faster for us.

I see Sissy narrow her eyes, and when
I leap into the air she shouts, "No. 1, your
bom-bom is still white!"

I twist in the air to take a look at my
bottom, and everybody laughs! Quickly I sit
down. Sissy smiles.

Now Mama Coca-Cola's new house is finished, the party is over, and life is as before. Coca-Cola and I are busy all day fetching and carrying, herding the goats, watering the cows, hoeing the fields, gathering palm nuts and carrying firewood. Mama, Grandmother and the aunties smile to see us work so hard. They say they are giving us all these jobs to help us rebuild our muscles after all that sitting down.

But there is one thing that is not as before. When I look towards the iroko tree, there is somebody sitting in my place next to Grandfather. It is Mama Coca-Cola. Ever since she moved to her new house, she has stopped frying akara and started sitting under the iroko tree.

"Your mother is under the iroko tree,"
I say to Coca-Cola one day when we are in
the bush.

He shrugs.

"Does she not have akara to fry?" I ask.

"She is tired," Coca-Cola says.

I frown at Coca-Cola. Mama Coca-Cola
is never tired.

When we return to the village, I allow my
legs to wander close to the iroko tree. I can
hear Mama Coca-Cola's voice. "That iron
roof like oven. OVEN! I tell you. All night I
am sweating! Sweating! And come morning
I have headache. BIG headache."

Grandfather shakes his head sorrowfully
and waves his fly whisk.

"I cannot fry akara. My headache is too
big," continues Mama Coca-Cola. "And I
cannot even lie in my own house because it
is hot-hot-hot. I have to sit here in the shade
and watch my business die!"

Mama Coca-Cola starts to cry. Then
Coca-Cola starts to cry. Sunshine and Smile,
sitting at their mother's feet, start to cry. The
women come out of their compounds and
gather around Mama Coca-Cola.

"That house is dirty! Dirty! No matter
how many times I sweep, every time I
look in corner I find dust! And Coca-Cola is
coughing-coughing all night."

I look at Coca-Cola. "Why did you not tell
me?" I ask.

Coca-Cola shrugs.

"In a round house, dust will not stay," says
Mama. "But where there is corner, there is
dust."

"This is very bad," says Grandmother.

"But it is worse. Look at my babies!"
Mama Coca-Cola cries.

Mama Coca-Cola holds up Sunshine and
Smile. They are covered in angry red bites.

"Mosquitoes love my house!" Mama

Coca-Cola wails. "They love it too much!"

"This is not good!" cries Grandmother. "Your babies will become sick!"

"It is very bad." Mama Coca-Cola weeps.

Nobody knows what to say. This is terrible. Mama Coca-Cola's new house has taken her money, and now it is taking the health of her and her children.

A BMW races past the abandoned akara stall, splashing it with water from the road. One of the crates falls over into the mud.

Mama Coca-Cola weeps louder when she sees this. Mama tries to comfort her.

"When you are back in business, everybody will stop and buy," she says.

"Nobody with money ever stopped to buy from me," Mama Coca-Cola cries. "Rich people, they all want chop-house restaurant. They like to sit on chair, to enjoy four walls and roof."

I look down at the akara stall. It is three upturned crates normally piled high with plates of akara. In the rainy season Mama Coca-Cola covered the plates with plastic to protect them from the rain. In the dry season she used a small leafy branch to wave flies from the plates. Nobody ever stopped there who was not happy to squat on the ground while they ate.

"It was not a good business anyway," Mama Coca-Cola sobs.

Everybody looks worried. Will Mama Coca-Cola abandon her business forever?

Another car races along the road. It is the Firebird. I am too sad for Mama Coca-Cola to shout out. The Firebird slows down by Mama Coca-Cola's new house and then speeds up again. The professor probably mistook the new house for one of those fancy chop-house restaurants that rich people love so much.

This triggers electricity for brain! I am on my feet. "Chop-house! Chop-house!" I shout.

Everybody looks at me as if I have gone crazy. Uncle Go-Easy, who was squatting, falls over in the dust. Mama tries to shush me. Grandmother scowls. Mama Coca-Cola is still crying.

I run down to the road. I take a big stick and point to the walls of Mama Coca-Cola's house. I shout loud so that everybody under the iroko tree can hear me.

"Four walls!" I say, "Like chop-house."

Grandfather stands up. He shades his eyes and looks towards the house.

I point to the roof.

"Roof!" I shout. "To protect customers from sun and rain."

Mama Coca-Cola is now standing too. And Mama and the aunties and even Uncle Go-Easy. They are all staring at the house.

I point to the concrete floor through the open door.

"Concrete floor!" I shout. "To support tables and chairs for those who do not like to squat on the ground."

Suddenly Mama Coca-Cola is running towards the house. The whole village is following her. When she reaches the house her eyes are wide. I point to the ground where I am standing, next to the house.

"Shade," I say quietly, "for somebody to fry akara out of the hot-hot sun."

Mama Coca-Cola closes her eyes. "But if this is a chop-house, where will I and my children sleep?"

"In my house," says Mama B quickly. "You must return to my house."

"And when the rainy season is over, we will build you a new house," says Grandfather.

"A traditional house," says Grandmother loudly, "with no corner for the dirt to gather. Palm frond roof and thick clay wall to keep the house cool and quiet."

"And traditional plaster that soothes the eyes and repels the mosquito," says Uncle Go-Easy.

Mama Coca-Cola smiles and then laughs. Then she shouts, "Coca-Cola! Run for town! Tell sign painter to come here. Tell him I want red, yellow, green and plenty-plenty words."

Mama Coca-Cola looks at the village. "I need table. I need chair. You must lend them to me, and I will return them when I have money to buy my own," she says. "When I return them, I will buy everybody one new chair."

The aunties groan.

"First our buckets, now our tables and chairs," Grandmother says crossly.

But everybody goes to their houses and carries any tables or chairs they own down to the new chop-house. Everybody wants a rich BMW businessman or Mercedes Benz chief to sit on their chair or eat at their table.

Now only three days later we have a brand-new modern chop-house on the road outside our village. For those who can read, the sign says:

No.1 CHOP HOUSE
Famous for Akara

The smell of frying akara speaks to those who can't read.

In the shade near the door, Mama Coca-Cola is frying akara and chatting to those customers who prefer to squat outside in the traditional way.

Next to them are parked BMWs and Mercedes Benz. The owners are enjoying akara inside. Sitting on chairs and eating at tables which were in our own houses not so long ago.

"Firebird!" shouts Coca-Cola.

The Firebird stops right outside the chop-house. The professor climbs out. He is holding a newspaper. He enters the chop-house. Coca-Cola comes running up to the iroko tree.

"The prof!" he shouts. "The prof is looking for you!"

I look at Grandfather. He looks at me. Then Grandfather stands up under the iroko tree and brushes the dirt from his clothes. He walks stiffly down to the road. Grandfather enters the chop-house. Coca-Cola and I look through the window. The professor greets Grandfather. They look at the paper the professor is holding. Grandfather smiles.

"No. 1!" he shouts.

I enter the chop-house. On the front of the newspaper is a photograph of me leading the Cow-rolla loaded with passengers through the flood!

"It seems I left too early and missed the fun." The professor smiles at me.

I smile back my biggest smile. Then I look out of the window at the Firebird. It is so close! The professor puts the paper down.

He laughs. "You are more interested in my car than your own celebrity photograph!"

I nod my head. The professor laughs again.

"Let us eat some of this famous akara!" he says. "I want to hear more about your ideas. Then I will take you for a ride in my car."

I smile a big-big smile.

I am the No. 1. The No. 1 car spotter in the world. I can eat akara with a university professor, no problem!

Then I am going to jump into the fabulous Pontiac Firebird! I am the No. 1 car spotter – now watch me cruise in the No. 1 car!

Atinuke was born in Nigeria
and spent her childhood in both Africa
and the UK. She tells traditional African
tales in schools, theaters and storytelling
festivals all over the world. *The No. 1 Car
Spotter and the Firebird* is her seventh book.
Atinuke lives with her husband and two
young sons in Wales.

Warwick Johnson Cadwell lives
by the Sussex seaside with his smashing
family and pets. Most of his time is
spent drawing or thinking about drawing,
but for a change of scenery he also
skippers boats.